LOOK!
THERE'S A
GHOST

Can you spot them all?

igloobooks

MEET THE GHOSTS!

Time to get spooky! Ten ghosts are hiding on every page in this fun book. Read the profiles below to learn all about their haunting personalities, then look carefully at the scenes to find where each one is hiding. Answers are at the back of the book so you can check your ghost-searching skills!

BOO

KNOWN FOR:
Being the first to boogie at a party

FAVORITE GADGET:
Headphones

FAVORITE GAME:
Chase

BLAIR

FAVORITE SPORT:
Soccer

FAVORITE THING TO WEAR:
Soccer team scarf

LIKES:
Scoring ghouls

SABRINA

MOST-EATEN SNACK:
Cheese on ghost

KNOWN FOR:
Looking fab-oo-lous

LOVES:
Fairground roller-ghosters

CARRIE

KNOWN FOR:
Always being in good spirits

FAVORITE THING TO WEAR:
Pink bow

MOST-USED PHRASE:
That's spook-tacular!

FRANKIE

FAVORITE TREAT:
Ice scream

MOST-LOVED ACCESSORY:
Spook-tacles

MOST-USED PHRASE:
Creep it real!

DANA

FAVORITE FOOD:
Spook-ghetti Bolognese

FAVORITE THING TO DO:
Haunt people

FAVORITE COLOR:
Red

CAIN

KNOWN FOR:
Being really ghoul

FAVORITE FILMS:
Scary ones

FAVORITE THING TO DO:
Trick-or-treat!

THEO

MOST-LOVED ACCESSORY:
Purple neckerchief

FAVORITE KIND OF SNACK:
Boo-scuits

FAVORITE THING TO DO:
Ghost walks

BONNIE

BESTIE:
Dana

BEST FEATURE:
Her hair

FAVORITE BEAUTY PRODUCT:
Scare spray

SAUL

FAVORITE FRUIT:
Straw-boo-ries

FAVORITE FILM:
Paddington Scare

FAVORITE FOOD:
Pumpkin pie

SPOOKY SEARCH

The ghosts love haunting this creepy mansion.
Can you find all ten hiding in this spooky scene?

CAN YOU SPOT THE ONLY PURPLE BAT?

FARMYARD FRIGHTS

Scarecrows aren't the only scary things on this farm!
Can you find where the ten ghosts are hiding?

CAN YOU SPOT
THE ONLY
PINK OWL?

GALACTIC GHOSTS

Search this space scene to find the hiding
places of each of the ten ghosts.

CAN YOU SPOT THE ONLY PINK MOON?

A FUNFAIR SCARE

The ghosts are ready to have a great time at the fair.
Can you find all ten of them among the rides?

ENJOY THE RIDES!

CAN YOU SPOT THE GREEN PUMPKIN?

PEEKABOO!

Ten ghosts have traveled deep into the jungle.
But where are they all hiding?

CAN YOU SPOT THE BLACK CAT?

TRICK-OR-TREAT?

There are plenty of treats to be found on this page.
Can you find all ten ghosts, too?

CAN YOU SPOT
THE ORANGE
FROG?

BIG SCREEN SCREAM

Everyone is waiting for the film to start.
Can you find the ten ghosts who are ready to scare?

CAN YOU SPOT THE PURPLE CANDY APPLE?

WATER FRIGHT!

Some of the ghosts like to swim! Try to find
all ten ghouls in this busy scene.

CAN YOU SPOT THE LITTLE RED BUG?

COOL GHOULS

The ghost friends love hanging out at the park.
Look very carefully to track down all ten ghosts.

CAN YOU SPOT THE PURPLE AND ORANGE KITE?

TOY TROUBLE

Not everything in this shop is a toy!
Check everywhere to find the silly ghosts.

CAN YOU SPOT THE WITCH'S BROOMSTICK?

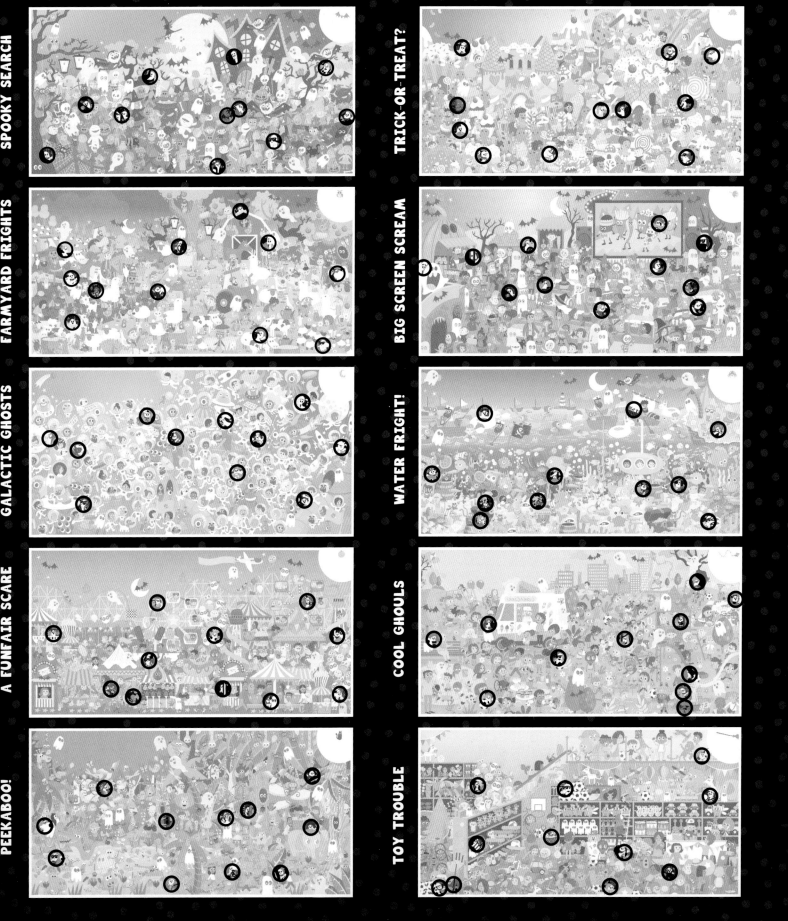

SPOOKY SEARCH

TRICK-OR-TREAT?

FARMYARD FRIGHTS

BIG SCREEN SCREAM

GALACTIC GHOSTS

WATER FRIGHT!

A FUNFAIR SCARE

COOL GHOULS

PEEKABOO!

TOY TROUBLE